Pony-Crazed Princess

A Surprise for Princess Ellie

Read all the adventures of Princess Ellie!

Pony-Crazed Princess

A Surprise for Princess Ellie

by Diana Kimpton

Illustrated by Lizzie Finlay

Hyperion Paperbacks for Children
New York

For Caitlin

First published in the United Kingdom in 2004 as
The Pony-Mad Princess: A Surprise for Princess Ellie
by Usborne Publishing Ltd.
Based on an original concept by Anne Finnis
Text copyright © 2004 by Diana Kimpton and Anne Finnis
Illustrations copyright © 2004 by Lizzie Finlay

Printed in the United States of America
First U.S. edition, 2007
1 3 5 7 9 10 8 6 4 2

This book is set in 14.5-point Nadine Normal.

ISBN 0-7868-4875-8

Visit www.hyperionbooksforchildren.com

Chapter 1

"Good girl," said Princess Ellie, as she cantered Moonbeam toward the last jump. The palomino pony eyed the wooden poles and tried to swerve away. But Ellie was prepared for that. She kept a firm hold on the reins and pushed the pony on with her legs. Moonbeam did as she was told. She leaped forward and cleared the jump easily.

Ellie galloped across the finish line and

pulled her pony to a halt. Then she turned around to see how the others were doing.

She was just in time to watch her best friend soar over the wooden poles on Rainbow. Kate's jumping had improved enormously since she had come to live with her grandmother, the palace cook. Perhaps that was because of all the practice she had been having on Ellie's ponies.

Prince John, riding Sundance, was farther back. The chestnut pony jumped over a fallen tree trunk and cantered down the hill toward the last jump. He pricked his ears, lifted his front legs, and bounded over it. Prince John grinned broadly. It was hard to tell which of them was enjoying themselves more, as they rode to the end of the course.

"That was so much fun," said John as they rode slowly back toward the stable. "I'm going to ask my father for a cross-country course with lots of jumps on the grounds of our palace—but I'm sure mine will be longer."

"Of course it will," sighed Ellie. She really liked John. He was the only royal person she knew who shared her love of ponies. But he did have an annoying habit of insisting that everything was bigger and better at his palace in Andirovia.

Kate leaned forward and patted Rainbow's gray neck. "I'm not surprised you want one," she said. "Cross-country's much more exciting than jumping in the paddock."

"But even that's not as exciting as going on a real adventure," said John. "Do you remember how we went hunting for ghosts the last time I came to visit?"

"I remember being really scared," said Ellie.

"So do I," agreed Kate.

"But it was still fun," laughed John. "So what are we going to look for this time?" The girls stared at him blankly. "Well, aren't there any mysterious legends about your palace? No stories of hidden treasure?"

"I've never heard of any," said Ellie.

"Dragon's eggs?" asked John.

"Now you're just being silly," giggled Kate.

"Come on. Not even a secret passage?" suggested John. "All the best palaces have one of those. The one we have at home is really cool."

"But that's not secret," Ellie declared. "It can't be a secret if you know about it."

At that moment, they reached the path that led to the palace stable. A bay pony whinnied loudly and cantered across the nearby field to meet them. She was larger than the ponies they were riding, and the long hair that nearly hid her hooves made her look like a miniature cart horse. She skidded to a halt beside the fence and put her head over the top rail to greet the riders.

"This is Starlight," explained Ellie, as Moonbeam sniffed noses with the bay pony. "Do you like her?"

"She's a beauty," said John. It was the first time he had come to visit Ellie since Starlight had arrived, so he hadn't met her before. "She looks much better than she did in that photo you e-mailed to me."

Ellie smiled proudly. "That photo was

taken before I'd had a chance to clean her up. She'd been living wild for so long that she looked really neglected."

"Well, she doesn't anymore," said John. He twisted a finger thoughtfully in Sundance's chestnut mane and added, "She's really fat now, actually."

"No, she's not," said Ellie, indignantly. "She's just well built, that's all. Ponies like her have big bones." She turned Moonbeam away from the fence and led the way toward the stable. "You don't have to be thin to be beautiful."

There was a long, awkward pause. Then Kate got a wistful look on her face. "I wish I could find a pony," she said.

"So do I," said John. "I'd like a palomino, like Moonbeam."

"Copycat!" cried Ellie.

"Am not!" said John. "My palomino would be bigger than yours."

"Then it wouldn't be like Moonbeam," Ellie declared. "Anyway, you don't need another pony. You already have two." She'd seen plenty of pictures of the beautiful chestnut mares he'd left behind in Andirovia.

"Why shouldn't I have three?" argued John. "You already had Sundance, Moonbeam, Rainbow, and Shadow when you got Starlight. That's five." He shrugged his shoulders. "Anyway, there's no point arguing about it. My father already thinks I spend too much time riding. There's no way he'd buy me another pony."

"My dad won't get me a pony at all," added Kate, very quietly.

The sadness in her voice made Ellie feel guilty. It was mean of her to argue with John about how many ponies they each had, when Kate didn't even have one. Ellie was happy to share her ponies with her best friend, but she knew that it wasn't the same. Kate desperately wanted a pony of her own. If only there were something Ellie could do to help.

Chapter 2

The stable was deserted when Ellie, John, and Kate rode in. There was no sign of Meg, the palace groom, but she had left the ponies' stalls ready for them. Each one had a thick bed of sweet-smelling straw, a bulging hay net, and a bucket of clean water. The three friends led the ponies inside, took off their saddles and bridles, and brushed their backs carefully. Then they left them alone to have a quiet, well-earned rest.

Ellie was just rinsing Moonbeam's bit under the tap when Shadow, her black Shetland, trotted into the yard. He was pulling a carriage with Great-Aunt Edwina in the driver's seat, and he looked very proud of himself. He carried his head high as his tiny hooves clattered on the cobbles.

Great-Aunt Edwina pulled him to a halt and announced, "That was a wonderful drive. We went right around the deer park, just as I used to when I was a girl."

She waited while Kate ran over and took hold of Shadow's bridle. Then she climbed down slowly to the ground, her long skirt rustling as she moved. "You children are probably looking forward to the party tomorrow."

"That's why my family came to visit," said John. "We didn't want to miss it—although I'm sure it won't be as exciting as our parties in Andirovia."

"Yes, it will!" declared Ellie. "It's going to be great. There'll be music and dancing and jugglers and magicians and everything."

"It'll be the best party ever," cried Kate, her voice filled with enthusiasm. She wasn't usually allowed to attend royal events.

"Imagine your parents celebrating their crystal jubilee," sighed Great-Aunt Edwina. "I can't believe it's been fifteen years since they became King and Queen. It seems like their coronation was only yesterday. Time goes so much faster now than it did when I was a little girl."

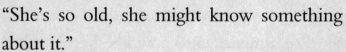

John moved next to Ellie and nudged her hard in the ribs. "Ask her about the secret passage," he whispered. "She's so old, she might know something about it."

"I might be old, but I am not deaf," said Great-Aunt Edwina, sternly. "Why don't you ask me yourself?"

John's ears turned pink with embarrassment. He bowed politely. "We were just wondering whether there's a secret passage in the palace. We have one in ours."

To Ellie's delight, her great-aunt immediately replied, "That's not very secret, is it? It can't be if you know about it." John's ears grew even pinker as the old lady continued. "Our passage really is secret. I searched and searched for it when I was a girl, but I was never able to find it."

"So, how do you know it's there?" asked Ellie, with a surge of excitement. Maybe John was right. Maybe they could have an adventure after all.

"I read about it in my history books," explained Great-Aunt Edwina. "It's called the Angel Pathway. Old King Liam had it built to help him escape from danger, but he never told anyone else where it was." The old lady sighed and walked up to the black Shetland pony. She stroked his nose and gave him his favorite treat—a peppermint. Then she waved good-bye and headed back toward the palace.

John waited until she had gone a safe distance before speaking again. "I told you there's a secret passage," he said with a triumphant grin.

Ellie grinned back. "Okay! You win! Now, stop gloating, and help me unharness Shadow."

She bent down and unhooked the long leather straps that attached the Shetland to the carriage. Then she and John slid the shafts out of the leather loops on either side of the harness.

"I'll take care of the rest," called Kate, as she led the Shetland into his stall.

Ellie stepped forward to help, but then she changed her mind. Maybe it would be better to let Kate do it by herself, she thought. Then Kate could pretend Shadow was hers if she wanted to. It might make her feel better about not having a pony of her own.

Just then, Meg led Starlight into the yard. Ellie looked carefully at the bay mare. Perhaps her tummy did stick out a bit further than it used to. But that still didn't mean that John was right. "Starlight's not fat, is she?" asked Ellie, hoping Meg would agree with her.

But Meg didn't agree. Instead, she sighed and ran her hand over the pony's bulging side. "She is getting a big belly."

"I told you so," said John.

Ellie ignored him. She was more concerned with Starlight. "Is that unhealthy?" she asked.

"I don't think so," replied Meg. "But just in case, I'll ask the vet to look at her next time he comes to the palace."

The mention of the vet threw Ellie into a panic. Suppose he found something wrong with Starlight? Ellie couldn't bear the thought of anything happening to her newest pony.

Chapter 3

Ellie was very quiet as she walked back to the palace with John and Kate. "I'm worried about Starlight," she explained, when they asked what she was thinking about.

"We all are," said Kate. "I wish there was something we could do for her. But we just have to wait for the vet."

"And he's not coming until after the party," added John, "so let's forget about it for now. We've got a secret passage to find."

Ellie smiled. For once, she was willing to admit that he was right. Searching for the Angel Pathway was just what she needed to keep her mind off the matter of Starlight's health. "When should we start?" she asked.

"Now," said John. "There's just enough time before dinner."

Kate shook her head. "I can't. My dad's supposed to call later, and I don't want to miss him." Her parents worked abroad and moved around a lot. That was why she stayed with her grandparents, who worked at the palace. That way she avoided having to keep changing schools.

"Then it's just the two of us," said John, looking at Ellie. "But we'd better get changed for dinner before we start."

Ellie waved good-bye to Kate and raced up the spiral staircase to her very pink bedroom. As soon as she was inside, she tore off her dirty riding clothes and replaced them with a much less comfortable pink dress with silver bows and matching silver sandals. Then she gave her face a quick wash, swapped her everyday crown for her second-best tiara, and ran downstairs again.

John was already there, but before he had time to say anything, Miss Stringle came bustling into view. "I've been looking everywhere for you, Princess Aurelia."

Ellie groaned. She hated being called by

her real name, and she suspected that the arrival of her governess would put a damper on her plans with John. Miss Stringle had strict ideas on the way princesses should behave. She certainly wouldn't approve of Ellie's searching for secret passages.

Miss Stringle ignored Ellie's reaction and curtsied to John. "I've just been talking to your parents, Your Highness. The Emperor and Empress have agreed that you can help Princess Aurelia give everyone a surprise at tomorrow's celebration."

"Are we going to jump out of a cake?" cried Ellie. She'd seen someone do that once on television, and it had looked like a lot of fun.

"Absolutely not," said her governess in a horrified voice. "That's far too undignified for a prince and princess. You are going to sing a song together. Now, come to the schoolroom quickly. You must start practicing right away."

The song was better than Ellie had expected. It had a catchy tune, and the words were easy to learn. "Can Kate sing with us?" she asked during rehearsal. "It would sound so much better with three of us."

"Of course she can't," said Miss Stringle. "This is a royal surprise, and Kate is not royal."

Ellie scowled. She hated it when her governess looked down on Kate. "But she's my friend," argued Ellie.

"And mine," added John.

"That makes no difference," said Miss

Stringle, firmly. "She is only the cook's granddaughter, and she is not taking part in the surprise."

Her attitude took the energy out of their singing and made the rest of the rehearsal drag past slowly. Ellie found it hard to concentrate. When she wasn't worrying about Starlight, she was worrying about Kate. It seemed unfair that Kate should be left out of the performance, when she already had to put up with not being able to see her parents every day and not having a pony.

Dinnertime dragged just as slowly. Ellie and John wanted to finish as quickly as possible so that they could start looking for the Angel Pathway. But the King and Queen were obviously not in a hurry, and neither were John's parents. Ellie had never in her life seen four people eat so slowly. They slowly nibbled their smoked salmon and roast turkey. Then they lingered over their strawberry meringue cake.

Ellie swallowed the last of her meringue cake and waited impatiently for them to stop talking. So did John. He fidgeted from side to side and drummed his feet on the legs of his chair. Then he picked up a silver spoon and tried to balance it on his nose. Ellie stifled a giggle. She licked her finger and began to run it round and round the rim of her crystal glass. The glass started to hum—a single, high-pitched note that grew louder as she moved her finger faster and faster.

"Aurelia!" hissed the Queen. "That is no way for a royal person to behave."

"Neither is that," groaned the Emperor, staring at the spoon that was now hanging from the end of John's nose.

"You'd better excuse yourself from the table, Aurelia," sighed the King. "Take John with you, and find something sensible to do."

"But, please, make it nothing to do with ponies," said the Emperor. He was irritated by John's love of ponies. He would have preferred for his son to like boats.

Ellie and John left the room as quickly as they could. "Let's start the search up here," said John, leading the way up a narrow staircase to the next floor.

"What exactly are we looking for?" asked Ellie.

"Hollow walls, secret door handles, stuff like that," said John. He turned left into a corridor and pointed at the wooden panels that lined the walls. "I bet you the passage is somewhere behind that." He started to walk along the wall, knocking on the wood. "The area with the secret door will sound different when you knock it."

Ellie followed his example. She worked her way along the opposite wall, without success. Every knock sounded as dull and uninteresting as the one before it. There was no sign of anything unusual until they reached the landing. From there, a large, impressive staircase curved its way down to the main entrance hall. The top of the banister ended in a carved wooden post, and the top of the post was decorated with a glittering, golden ball.

"That looks just like a giant doorknob," cried Ellie. She grabbed hold of it with both hands and tried to turn it. The ball moved very slightly. She tried again, heaving with all her strength. This time, the ball turned.

"Keep going," said John. "I bet it opens a secret door."

But it didn't. As Ellie twisted the ball around and around, it gradually unscrewed itself from the top of the post. Suddenly, it came free and wobbled out of her fingers.

Ellie tried to grab it, but she was too late.

The golden ball fell to the ground and rolled rapidly down the stairs, glittering in

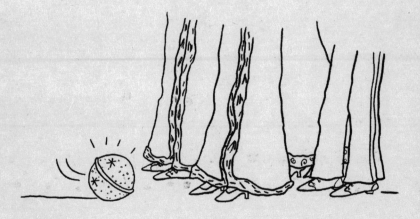

the light from the chandelier as it thudded from step to step. Ellie and John raced after the ball, but it was going too fast. It reached the bottom before they did, and came to a halt in front of four pairs of feet.

"Oh, no," groaned Ellie. The feet belonged to the King and Queen, and to the Emperor and Empress of Andirovia. This time she was really in trouble.

Chapter 4

The King and Queen stared at the golden ball in surprise. So did the Emperor and Empress. Ellie's mind raced as she wondered how she would talk her way out of this.

"Ouch!" cried the King, as he tried to kick the extremely hard ball out of his way. "What is the meaning of this, Aurelia?"

"I . . . um . . . we . . . uh . . ." For once, Ellie was completely at a loss for words.

Luckily, John wasn't. "I'm very sorry. It was entirely my idea." He batted his eyelashes at his parents in an expression of complete innocence. "You asked us to find something that had nothing to do with ponies. So I suggested soccer. And that's the only ball we could find."

To Ellie's amazement, they believed him. The Emperor nodded approvingly. "Soccer is a manly sport," he said.

"I'm surprised you can still walk," said the King. He stood on one foot, slipped off his other shoe, and rubbed his bruised toes gently on the back of his leg.

"You'll find a much softer ball in the royal gym," suggested the Queen. She glanced at

Ellie with a hint of suspicion in her eyes. "I'm surprised you didn't think of that yourself, Aurelia."

Ellie led John away quickly, before her mother had time to ask any questions. It seemed safest to head in the direction of the royal gym and get out of sight as soon as possible.

Suddenly, John stopped. "That's it!" he cried, pointing at a statue of an angel that stood on a ledge halfway up the wall.

"Huh? That's what?" asked Ellie.

The statue had been there for as long as she could remember, and it looked exactly the same as it always had.

"The way into the secret passage, of course," said John. "I bet the statue is the lever that opens the door. That would explain why it's called the Angel Pathway."

"Should I pull it?" squealed Ellie, her eyes bright with excitement.

"No, I'll do it!" said John. "I have more experience with secret passages than you do." He stood up on tiptoe, grabbed the statue with both hands, and pulled the top of it down toward him.

The stone angel tipped slowly forward. Ellie glanced around, looking for a secret door. Then she looked back just in time to see the angel tip over and tumble off its shelf. It landed on John's head, before bouncing onto the floor.

"Ow," said John, rubbing the top of his

head in pain. "Is it okay?"

"I think so," said Ellie, peering at the top of his head. "I can't see any swelling."

John pushed her away. "I meant, the angel."

Ellie looked down and sighed with relief. The statue was still in one piece. John's head and the thick carpet had broken its fall. But there was no sign of a secret door. The statue wasn't a lever after all.

"That's okay," said John, brightly. "We'll be right next time—the third time's the charm."

"It's getting late. We'd better wait until tomorrow," said Ellie. They'd already had two disasters, and she had a feeling that it wasn't only good luck that came in threes.

But there was no chance to look for secret passages the next morn- ing. The palace was bustling as everyone prepared for the jubilee party. Maids were polishing the silver until it gleamed. Footmen were putting up balloons everywhere. And gardeners were bringing in armfuls of flowers. No one wanted the children getting in the way.

So, Ellie and John put on their riding clothes, grabbed their backpacks, and went happily to the stable.

Kate was waiting for them with three packed lunches. "My grandmother made these for us. She said we should stay out of everyone's way until the party starts."

"Let's go for a picnic ride," suggested Ellie. "I'll take Starlight." She knew she'd be less likely to worry about the bay mare if she took her out for a ride.

"That's not a good idea," said Meg. "I don't think you should ride her until the vet says she's okay."

Ellie's panic returned. "What's wrong with her?" she asked.

Meg smiled reassuringly. "Don't worry! I'm sure it's nothing serious. I just have a feeling, that's all. And if I'm right, you shouldn't be riding her."

"What kind of feeling?" asked Ellie.

"I'm not going to tell you," said Meg. "I don't want you to be disappointed if I'm wrong."

Ellie looked at Meg in surprise. What was the matter with Starlight? she wondered. And why did Meg insist on being so secretive about it?

Chapter 5

Ellie was still puzzling over Meg's words as they set out on the ride. But gradually, the pleasure of riding Moonbeam pushed her worries to the back of her mind. She cantered across the deer park with Kate and Rainbow on one side of her and John and Sundance on the other. They all turned uphill into the woods, twisting and turning among the trees until they came out on an open hilltop—the perfect place to eat.

They dismounted and ate their lunch there, overlooking the sea. It was great to be far from the palace with no one around, just the ponies and a few sheep grazing on the grass.

"Let's go to the beach," suggested John, as he gave his apple core to Sundance.

"That's a great idea," said Kate. "But is there time before the party?"

"Sure there is," said Ellie. "We don't have to stay long."

The path down the cliff was steep and stony. The ponies' hooves slithered and slid on the pebbles as they picked their way down. Ellie was glad when they reached the beach and the stones disappeared. Ahead of them lay a huge stretch of soft, white sand.

"Oh, the tide's out," said Kate, sounding disappointed. "The sea is so far away I can hardly see it."

"We can't wade in the surf," moaned Ellie.

"But we can explore," said John. "We can ride out to that headland. We'd never be able to reach it at high tide."

Ellie looked in the direction he was pointing and saw that he was right. On the other side of the beach, the cliff curved gracefully and headed out toward the sea, ending in a dramatic tumble of rocks. But there was no water around them today. The tide was so far out that the rocks were dry.

"Come on," called John. "There's got to be all sorts of exciting things out there." He turned Sundance toward the headland and urged the chestnut pony into a gallop. Ellie and Kate raced after him on their horses. The ponies' tails streamed behind them in the wind as their hooves pounded across the damp sand. Ellie leaned forward over Moonbeam's snow-white mane, enjoying the excitement of the gallop.

When they reached the headland, they slowed the ponies to a walk. "That was fun," said Ellie, patting the palomino's neck. Then

she spotted something strange at the bottom
of the cliff. It was a huge, dark shape
that looked like a giant's mouth.

John had seen it, too.
He trotted Sundance
toward it and yelled,
"It's a cave!"

Ellie and Kate
followed him and
peered through the
opening. The cave
was even larger inside than
it looked on the outside. They couldn't see
to the back at all. The floor sloped up gently
from the entrance and disappeared into the
darkness.

"Let's explore it," said John. He urged
Sundance into the cave, obviously expecting

the others to follow his lead.

"No!" said Kate, with a shudder. "It looks scary. I don't want to go in there."

"Neither do I," said Ellie, happy that she wasn't the only one who was frightened.

"But we might find some hidden treasure," pleaded John from inside.

"Or something worse," said Kate. "Bats live in caves . . . and so do dragons."

John put his hand to his mouth and shouted, "Hello! Is anyone there?" His words echoed around the cave, bouncing back at him from the distant walls. But there was no other answer—no sound of scrabbling claws or flapping wings. "See?" he said. "It's completely empty."

"I still don't want to go inside," Ellie said firmly. "And I think you should come out."

John looked so disappointed that, for a moment, she thought he might refuse.

But his enthusiasm returned when she suggested they look for rock pools instead. Kate agreed that that would be a much safer activity, and the three friends set off on the ponies once again.

They found a sheltered patch of sand just outside the cave and tied the ponies to some nearby rocks. Then they left Moonbeam, Sundance, and Rainbow to doze quietly in the sunshine while they set out to explore the rock pools.

Soon, Ellie, John, and Kate were climbing over the rocks, squealing with delight as they peered into the pools left behind by the tide. The water teemed with life. There were sea anemones, scuttling crabs, and tiny fish that swam so fast they were hard to spot.

There was so much to see that they completely lost track of time. They moved on from pool to pool, farther and farther from the waiting ponies.

Finally, they reached a tall, arched rock that marked the end of the headland. They decided to stop and rest for a few minutes.

"It looks like a giant doorway," said Kate, shading her eyes from the sun as she peered up at the arch.

Suddenly, they heard a dreadful sound. It was the squeal of a terrified horse.

Chapter 6

Ellie whirled around in horror. While they had been busy exploring, the tide had swept in, cutting off their route back to the shore. The low-lying sand they had cantered across earlier was completely covered with water, and the three ponies were trapped against the cliff, huddled together in terror. Moonbeam squealed again, as another wave hit the rocks and soaked her with spray.

Ellie started to clamber back across the rocks. "We have to save them!" she cried.

"And ourselves," John added in a serious voice.

Ellie looked around and saw what he meant. The rocky headland they were standing on was rapidly disappearing under the waves, too. Of course, Ellie thought. If there were rock pools, it meant the rocks must be submerged when the tide was in.

"Maybe we could swim to the beach," suggested John.

Ellie shook her head. "I don't think I can swim that far. I can only do two lengths of our pool. Although it is a very big pool," she quickly added, glancing over at John.

"We could climb up the arch," suggested Kate. "The top looks as if it never gets wet."

Ellie looked up and saw that she was right. The arch could save them, but it couldn't save the ponies. There had to be something else they could do.

Suddenly, Ellie had an idea. "We could take the ponies into the cave," she suggested. "We'll be safe in there."

"No!" cried Kate. "It'll fill up with water when the tide comes in."

"No, it won't," said John. "I've been inside. The floor slopes up, and the ground at the back is completely dry. We'll be safe if we go in far enough."

Ellie shuddered as she remembered how scary the cave had looked. But she pushed away her fear and declared, "Come on! It's the only way we can save the ponies."

They scrambled over the rocks, retracing

the route they had taken to reach the arch. But they were soon forced to give up. They couldn't get back the way they had come. Too many of the rocks were already under-water, and the waves sweeping across the others were threatening to knock the friends off their feet.

"We'll have to keep closer to the cliff," said John.

Ellie followed his lead, and, to her relief, she found a ledge of rock just wide enough to stand on. It jutted out from the face of the cliff and was still a few inches above the water. The three children edged carefully along it, with their backs against the cliff. They held hands to keep their balance and to give each other courage. Soon they were soaking wet from the icy-cold spray of the waves. The wind blew through their wet clothes and whipped the waves even higher.

Ellie sighed with relief as they jumped down on the other side. They quickly untied the frightened ponies and led them into the shelter of the cave. "It's all right now," whispered Ellie, stroking Moonbeam's neck. "We're safe here."

She smiled as she saw the terror fade

from the pony's eyes. If only her own fear would disappear as easily, she thought.

A wave broke and washed into the cave, swishing gently round their feet. The three friends led the ponies farther inside to find a good place to wait. It was close enough to the entrance that light still reached it, but far enough back to be dry and safe.

"I wonder how long we'll have to stay here," said Kate, as they sat huddled together on the cold rock floor.

"Probably a few hours," said John. "It'll take that long for the tide to go out again."

"Maybe we should talk about something else to pass the time," suggested Ellie. "Did your dad call last night, Kate?"

Her friend nodded miserably. "I asked him again about a pony, but he said no. He just doesn't understand how much I want one."

"I'm sorry," said Ellie. She knew there was nothing she could say that would help Kate, so she decided to change the subject. She glanced at her watch and groaned. "We're going to miss the party. I'll be in big trouble when we get back."

"So will I," said John. Then he grinned. "But at least we won't have to sing that song."

Kate looked confused, so John and Ellie told her about their rehearsal with Miss Stringle. To pass the time, they taught her the song. Singing helped drown out the sound of the waves, and it kept their minds off the danger—as did their loud crunching on the potato chips left over from lunch.

Eventually, however, they got tired of singing. Ellie and Kate sat in silence, staring dismally at the water and wishing it would go away. John was restless.

"I'm getting bored," he announced. "Let's explore."

Ellie eyed the darkness nervously and shook her head. "We can't—not without a light."

"I have a flashlight in my survival kit," said John.

"Your what?" asked Kate.

"My survival kit," repeated John, pulling a plastic box from his backpack. "All good explorers have one. I learned about it on the Internet."

Ellie was intrigued. She peered at the box and asked, "What's in it?"

John snapped open the lid proudly and pulled out the items inside it, one by one. "This is a piece of explorer-grade, extra-white chalk," he explained. "This is an explorer-grade, high-energy chocolate bar, specially designed to prevent starvation in the wilderness. This is a ball of explorer-grade string—it can lift an elephant out of a swamp without breaking."

"We won't need that," giggled Kate.

"There aren't any elephants around here."

John ignored her. "And this is my flashlight."

"Explorer-grade?" asked Ellie.

"Nope," said John. "Just waterproof, shockproof, and shatterproof." As he spoke, he switched it on and shone the beam of light around the cave.

Suddenly, he stopped and stared, his eyes wide with amazement. "Wow!" he yelled. "There's something over there—at the back of the cave."

Chapter 7

John ran into the darkness, taking the flashlight and Sundance with him. Moonbeam tried to follow, but Ellie held her back. Although John had convinced her that there were no dragons in the cave, she could think of plenty of other monsters that might be lurking in the shadows.

"Come on," called John. "You've got to see this."

"Is it alive?" Ellie asked nervously.

"No," said John.

"Are you sure?" said Kate.

"Of course I am," he replied, with growing impatience.

Ellie and Kate led their ponies cautiously toward the small patch of light. There were no monsters. John had found the entrance to a long, dark tunnel.

Ellie's fear was immediately replaced by curiosity. "Where do you think it goes?" she asked.

"Let's find out," suggested John. "Now that we've found a secret passage, we have to explore it."

Ellie grinned. Exploring the tunnel sounded much more exciting than sitting in the cave with nothing to do. There was just one problem. "What about the ponies? We can't leave them here on their own."

"We'll take them with us," declared John. "The tunnel's too low to ride through, but there's enough room to lead them."

Kate looked doubtful. "What if we get lost? I don't want to be trapped in there forever."

"That's why all good explorers need this," said John, pulling the chalk out from his survival kit. "If we draw crosses on the walls as we go along, we can easily find our way back if we need to."

He stepped into the tunnel, leading Sundance behind him. The chestnut pony followed happily, his ears pricked as if he were enjoying the adventure.

Moonbeam was less enthusiastic. She stared suspiciously at the hole in the wall and snorted through her nose. "There's nothing to be scared of," whispered Ellie, stroking the pony's neck. The palomino relaxed a little and stepped slowly through the entrance. The tunnel was narrower than Ellie had expected, forcing her to stay close to Moonbeam's head. But she didn't mind. The horse's warm, friendly scent helped to mask the smell of the damp, stale air.

"Is this the Angel Pathway?" asked Kate from her position at the back.

"It might be," said Ellie.

"But it might not," argued John. "I read on the Internet that secret passages near the sea are usually made by pirates or smugglers. It didn't say anything about kings."

They walked in silence for a long time, pausing every few minutes for John to chalk another cross on the wall. The farther they went in the cave, the more Ellie felt her initial enthusiasm disappear. She didn't like the narrow tunnel. She didn't like the echoing sound their footsteps made. And she especially didn't like the darkness that lurked beyond the beam of the flashlight.

"We should have been back at the stable by now," said Kate after a while. "Do you think they'll be worried about us?"

John pointed his flashlight at his watch and shook his head. "Not yet. They'll just be mad because we're late. The party must have started by now."

"I wish we were there," sighed Ellie.

"I wish we were anywhere but here," groaned Kate. "My feet hurt."

"Mine, too," said Ellie. "I feel as if we've been walking forever."

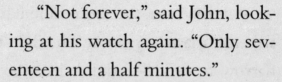

"Not forever," said John, looking at his watch again. "Only seventeen and a half minutes."

Ellie suddenly noticed that the light wasn't as bright as it had been before. "What's wrong with the flashlight?" she asked in alarm.

John shook the flashlight and groaned. "I think the batteries are starting to die."

"Shouldn't they have lasted

longer than that?" said Kate.

"Maybe you should have gotten explorer-grade ones," added Ellie.

John sighed. "I don't think I should have used it so much to make shadow puppets on my bedroom wall. Look—I can make a really good rabbit if I wiggle my fingers like this."

Ellie was not impressed. She just wanted to get out of the tunnel before the flashlight stopped working. "Will it last long enough to get us back to the front of the cave?" she asked.

"It should, if we hurry," said John. "Let's go."

Ellie tried to swing Moonbeam around to face the opposite way. But it was impossible.

The tunnel was too narrow. There wasn't enough room for the ponies to turn around. Ellie felt her stomach knot with fear. There was no way they could get back. They would have to keep walking into the unknown—and soon they would be doing it in the dark.

Chapter 8

Ellie, John, and Kate led the ponies through the tunnel as quickly as they could. They were desperate to find a way out before the flashlight's batteries died. Their fear grew stronger as the light got dimmer and dimmer. Ellie found herself thinking that this wasn't a very fun adventure. It was too scary.

"What if there isn't a way out?" cried Kate. She sounded very close to tears.

"There must be," said John. "Why would anyone build a secret passage that doesn't go anywhere?"

Ellie hoped he was right. She didn't mention her fear that the tunnel might be blocked by fallen rocks. There was no point in upsetting Kate even more. Instead, she stared at the ground, concentrating on her feet and trying to forget how close the walls were. As a result, she didn't notice that Sundance had stopped until she walked into his tail. The chestnut pony stamped his back foot in surprise and looked around to see what was happening.

"You can come closer," called John. "It's wider here."

Ellie and Kate led their ponies up beside him. John pointed the flashlight around the walls. "The walls are too smooth to be a cave," he said. "It must be some sort of secret room."

"I guess that's what you'd expect to find at the end of a secret passage," said Ellie. She looked around the room. Her eyes were wide.

"But there's no door," groaned Kate. "There's no way out. We're going to be trapped here forever!"

"No, we're not," said John. He was trying to be very calm. "There's room to turn the ponies here, so we can go back the way we came."

Ellie bit her lip nervously. The flashlight's batteries were now nearly dead, and she hated the idea of walking all the way back in the dark. She could tell that Moonbeam and the other ponies were starting to get a little afraid, too. There must be another solution, she thought. "Maybe there's a secret door," she suggested.

John moved the flashlight around the walls again. This time Ellie noticed that the wall at the far end looked even smoother than the others. She led Moonbeam over to it and ran her hands across its surface. "It's made of wood!" she yelled, with a note of triumph in her voice. "Maybe the whole wall is one big door."

John and Kate led their ponies over to examine the wall and started to search for a handle. At that moment, the flashlight went out completely, leaving them groping in the dark. Ellie's fingers closed on something smooth and round. She turned it as hard as she could and felt a wave of relief as she heard a loud click.

Light flooded in as the wall swung slowly open. It was dazzling after the darkness of the tunnel. Ellie closed her eyes for a moment to protect them. Then she opened them again and stared through the open doorway in surprise.

In front of her was the Grand Ballroom of the palace. The jubilee party was in full

swing, and the room was packed with people. The glittering light from the chandeliers made the ladies' diamond jewelry sparkle and the band's brass instruments gleam like gold. Maids ran up and down carrying trays of food, while music mingled with the sound of many voices talking at once.

The sound rapidly died away when the wall opened. Conversations stopped. Even the band stopped playing. Everyone stared at the mysterious opening in the wall and the strange, pony-shaped shadows lurking in the darkness.

Ellie spotted her parents just as they started to move toward the entrance to the tunnel. But she couldn't bear to wait for them to drag her out into the daylight. She would look like a naughty child in front of all those people. Worse still, she knew that this would probably ruin their party and their special day. There must be something she could do to make things right; if she could only think what it was.

Chapter 9

Ellie's mind raced as she tried to think. Then she had an idea. "Jump on quickly," she said to her friends. "There's only one thing we can do." She swung herself into Moonbeam's saddle and rode out through the opening to the small stage that stood in front of it. Then she smiled as brightly as she could and shouted, "Surprise!"

One of the maids was so shocked that she

let out a small scream and dropped her trays on the floor. Everyone else was equally surprised—but much less clumsy. Their mouths dropped open in astonishment at the sight of the three damp and dirty children riding through the opening in the ballroom wall on three equally damp and dirty ponies. They were even more amazed when they realized that two of the children were the prince and the princess. Everyone stared at Ellie and her friends. No one moved at all, except the maid, who was desperately trying to clean up the mess she had made.

"All together now," whispered Ellie. "On the count of three—one, two, three . . ."

Luckily, Kate and John had guessed what she planned to do. They joined in with her, singing Miss Stringle's song at the tops of their voices.

They sang all five verses perfectly. By the time they reached the end, the band had picked up the tune and joined in. They sang the chorus once more with the music before stopping.

At the end, the guests broke into applause. Some even cheered.

Miss Stringle did neither. She looked rather faint and had to be helped to a chair, where she sat sipping water from a crystal glass someone gave her and fanning herself with a napkin.

Great-Aunt Edwina climbed onto the stage with amazing agility for a lady of her age. "You found it!" she cried in great excitement.

"What do you mean?" asked Ellie.

"The Angel Pathway, of course." Edwina peered into the tunnel entrance and added, "I can't believe it was right here all along."

Ellie looked back at the secret door they had come through. On this side, it was disguised as an enormous painting of angels.

Suddenly everything made sense. It was the picture that had given the tunnel its name.

The guests clapped again as the King and Queen stepped onto the stage. The King raised his arms and waited for silence. Then he said, "I'm sure we are all delighted with my daughter's surprise entertainment. Now, please continue with the festivities, and enjoy yourselves."

He waved at the band to start playing again, and the guests went back to eating, talking, and dancing.

The Queen smiled at Ellie and her friends. "That was a lovely song, and such a surprise."

"It was certainly unexpected," added the King. He glanced over at Miss Stringle, who still hadn't recovered from her shock.

"Though I think maybe it didn't go quite as planned . . . but everything seems to have worked out all right in the end."

At that moment, there was a commotion at the door. Meg rushed in, wearing her stable clothes and looking nearly as out of place as Ellie and her friends among the beautifully dressed guests. She looked relieved when she saw Ellie. "Thank goodness you're here. I've been really worried about you." She stopped and scratched her head thoughtfully. "How did you get the ponies inside?"

"That's a very good question," said the

King. "But more to the point, how do you plan to get them out again?"

Ellie hadn't thought of that. Fortunately, John had. "We can go through there," he said, pointing across the ballroom to the French windows that led into the garden.

"And I suggest you do it as soon as possible," said the Queen. She smiled at a footman who had just arrived with a bucket and a shovel. "I don't think your ponies are housebroken."

Meg grinned. "There's another good reason for hurrying, but I'm not going to tell you what it is. You'll have to come back to the stable and see for yourselves. I want it to be a surprise."

Chapter 10

Ellie, John, and Kate rode the ponies across the ballroom and out through the French windows, followed closely by the footman with the bucket and another with a mop to clean up the wet hoofprints. They trotted to the yard as quickly as they could. They were anxious to see the surprise, but Meg made them wait until they had unsaddled Sundance, Moonbeam, and Rainbow and settled them in their stalls.

Then she led them across the yard and put her finger to her lips as she opened Starlight's door. The bay mare whinnied as they peered inside. But, to their amazement, she wasn't alone. Nestled in the straw was a beautiful newborn foal.

"Wow!" cried John and Kate in unison, their eyes wide with delight.

"He's gorgeous," said Ellie. She had never seen anything more wonderful in her whole life.

"He's a 'she,' actually," explained Meg, "and she came much sooner than I expected. I'd guessed Starlight was pregnant, but I didn't want to tell you until I'd checked with the vet."

"I've been so worried about her," laughed Ellie. "But now everything is absolutely perfect." She had fallen instantly in love with the foal and couldn't stop looking at her.

The foal wasn't a bay like her mother. She was a skewbald with pretty patches of brown and white hair. Her short mane stood straight up like a brush, and her tail was short and stubby.

Starlight whinnied again and nuzzled her

new baby. The foal responded by pushing against the ground with her wobbly front legs and trying to stand. It didn't work: when she was only halfway up, she lost her balance and tumbled onto her side.

"Oh, no!" gasped Ellie. "Is she hurt?"

Meg shook her head. "Don't worry. She'll be fine."

"Should we help?" asked Kate, anxiously. "Her legs are so long she doesn't seem to know what to do with them."

"Give her time," said Meg. "She'll learn. She just needs some practice."

They all held their breath as the foal tried again to stand. This time, she managed to get her front legs straight. It was the back ones that gave her trouble. When they were only halfway straightened, she slipped forward onto her knees. She rested for a moment, kneeling in the straw. Then she pushed up again with her front hooves; everyone gave a sigh of relief as she finally managed to stand.

Starlight proudly guided her baby's shaky steps until the foal was standing beside her.

"What are you going to call her?" asked the Queen, who'd left the party and come to the stables with the King.

Ellie jumped at the sound of her mother's voice. She had been so caught up in watching the foal that she hadn't noticed her parents arrive. They both looked very happy.

"What a surprise!" said the King, putting his arm around Ellie's shoulder. "You are a lucky girl. Imagine having six ponies."

Suddenly, Ellie thought of something. "I have a great idea," she whispered. "Can you both come outside so I can tell you?"

The King looked worried as he followed her into the yard. "Your ideas usually mean trouble, Aurelia." But as he listened to what Ellie whispered into his ear, he started to smile.

Then he whispered in the Queen's ear, and she smiled, too.

"For once I agree with you," said the

King, turning back to Ellie. "This time you really have thought of a brilliant idea."

"So you don't mind?" Ellie asked her parents.

"Not even a tiny bit," said the Queen. She gave Ellie a gentle kiss. "In fact, I'm proud of you for thinking of it."

When they went back into the stable, they found Kate stroking the foal's brown-and-white neck. "Isn't she just the sweetest thing?" she said. "She's a real angel."

"That would be a good name," said Ellie. "'Angel' would suit her."

"And it would remind us of our adventure," said John.

"But 'Jubilee' would remind us all of the day she was born," suggested the Queen.

"And 'Comet' would fit in with the other pony names," said the King. "They all have something to do with the sky."

"It sounds as if you've narrowed the choices down to three," said Meg. "Which is it going to be—Angel, Jubilee, or Comet? The choice is yours, Ellie."

"No, it's not," said Ellie. "It's up to Kate."

Kate looked up in surprise. "Why me?" she asked.

"Because she's your pony," said Ellie. "I

want you to have her."

Kate's surprise turned to shock. "You can't mean that."

"Yes, I can," said Ellie, firmly.

Kate ran over and hugged Ellie. "You're the best friend in the whole world."

"So are you," said Ellie, as she hugged Kate right back.

John sighed. "This lovey-dovey stuff is nice, but we still don't know the foal's name."

"She's Angel," said Kate. "My Angel."

"She sure is," said Ellie.

Pony-Crazed Princess

Collect all the books in this royally fun pony series!

by Diana Kimpton

HYPERION PAPERBACKS FOR CHILDREN

Available where books are sold